The Jiggery-Pokery Cup

Maybe I'll win six second prizes, thought Kelly. That would give me a good score.

But she knew she wouldn't. Rachel's cooking was better than hers; William would make a tidier model animal; and Flora had very elegant writing. They'd all get seconds and thirds when they didn't get firsts.

But I've got to beat them, thought Kelly. I really do want to win the Lady Jiggins-Povey Cup.

Angela Bull

The Jiggery-Pokery Cup

Illustrated by Pauline Hazelwood

Hippo Books
Scholastic Publications Limited
London

Scholastic Publications Ltd,
10 Earlham Street, London WC2H 9RX, UK

Scholastic Inc,
730 Broadway, New York, NY 10003, USA

Scholastic Tab Publications Ltd,
123 Newkirk Road, Richmond Hill,
Ontario L4C 3G5, Canada

Ashton Scholastic Pty Ltd,
P O Box 579, Gosford, New South Wales,
Australia

Ashton Scholastic Ltd,
165 Marua Road, Panmure, Auckland 6,
New Zealand

Text copyright © Angela Bull, 1990
Illustrations copyright © Pauline Hazelwood, 1990

First published 1990

ISBN 0 590 76189 7

Made and printed by Cox and Wyman Ltd,
Reading, Berks

Typeset in Baskerville by COLLAGE (Design in Print),
Longfield Hill, Kent

10 9 8 7 6 5 4 3 2 1

Chapter One

The sun was shining down on the Skelton Village Show. It twinkled on rows of cars, and bandsmen's gleaming trumpets. It touched the crowds of people streaming to and fro, the sweating horses, and the silky sheepdogs. It melted ice creams and candyfloss. It glowed through the white canvas of a big tent at one end of the field.

Inside the tent were several long tables, divided into sections with string. Each section contained the entries for a different competition. There were knitting and sewing classes, cakes, and jams, and homemade wine. The best ones had red cards beside them, saying "First Prize". There were blue cards for second prizes, and yellow cards for thirds.

One table was reserved for the children's classes, and that was where two boys were standing. Ben was twelve, with dark hair and clever black eyes. Jonathan was eight, with sandy hair and a freckled nose. For brothers, they weren't very alike, but just now their faces both looked the same — disappointed.

They had come into the tent to see if their sister, Kelly, had won any prizes. She had entered all the children's competitions, but the boys couldn't find her name on any of the coloured cards.

"Four butterfly buns. First Prize — Flora Sharp," read Jonathan. Flora's four buns, their sponge wings set jauntily in a swirl of cream, lay on a paper doily, with the red card tucked under its edge.

"Didn't Kelly even get second prize?" asked Ben.

He looked carefully, but the name Kelly Wigglesworth wasn't there. He moved on to the next section.

"Miniature flower arrangement. First Prize — Rachel Kitson," said the red card.

Miniature meant very small. Rachel had sliced the top off an eggshell, and filled it with tiny flowers, which spilled prettily down the sides.

"You've got to say that it's better than Kelly's," remarked Jonathan gloomily. He'd recognized Kelly's arrangement of pansies in a doll's cup, standing next to Rachel's eggshell. It looked untidy. There was a slapdash, impatient streak in Kelly, which, time and again, spoiled her chances.

"I wish she'd give up trying. She never wins anything," said Ben.

In the next section lay sheets of paper, with poems copied on to them.

"Handwriting Competition. First Prize — William Edge," read Ben.

"Kelly's entry looks terrible," said Jonathan, staring at their sister's uneven letters.

Ben was doing a quick count. "Rachel's got four first prizes, Flora's got three, William's got one and two seconds. Kelly's got nothing."

"As usual," sighed Jonathan. "But she won't give up." For one thing that could be said about Kelly was that she was determined. She wasn't very neat, or artistic, but she kept on trying.

"It's Grindlethorpe Show next week," said Ben. "That means the Lady Jiggins-Povey Cup."

Jonathan nodded.

Grindlethorpe was a nearby village. Ben, Kelly and Jonathan Wigglesworth lived there, and so did all the three prize-winners — Flora, Rachel and William. At Grindlethorpe Show, a beautiful silver cup was awarded to the child under eleven who won most competitions. Kelly had always longed to win the Cup, and since she was now ten, this year would be her last chance. Determination was all very well, but when Ben and Jonathan looked at her uneven writing, her untidy pansies, and her sprawling butterfly buns, they saw that she didn't have a hope.

Rachel and Flora came strolling down the tent to admire their coloured cards. Flora, in riding clothes with a hard hat under her arm, tossed her long hair, and looked sneeringly at Ben and Jonathan. Rachel was smiling like a cat with a saucer of cream — a kitty-cat, thought Ben. It really suited her to be called Kitson, just as it suited Flora to be called

Sharp.

"I've got four firsts. If this was Grindlethorpe Show I'd have won the Lady Jiggins-Povey Cup again," said Rachel.

"Only just," said Flora. "I've got three firsts and two seconds, and I won the Lady Jiggins-Povey Cup the year before you."

"William must have a bit of a chance of winning it," said Rachel. Her voice showed that she liked William.

"Not much. And he's only a baby of nine," returned Flora. She and Rachel, like Kelly, were ten.

"Poor Kelly's not been very lucky," said Rachel to Ben and Jonathan.

Ben was annoyed. He didn't want Rachel's sympathy.

"Kelly doesn't mind not winning," he snapped.

Flora gave her scornful laugh. "Everybody wants to win," she said.

It was true. Ben could only stare back at her in angry silence.

"Why don't you go in for some classes?" asked Rachel.

"Too old," said Ben.

"Too much hard work," said Jonathan.

"You wouldn't win, anyway," said Flora. "Wigglesworths never do."

"Pity there aren't any prizes for politeness," said Ben to Jonathan. "Come on, let's get a hotdog." And they stalked out of the

11

tent.

"It would be brilliant if Kelly could beat Flora and Rachel at Grindlethorpe Show," said Jonathan crossly.

"And that little wimp, William Edge. But she never will," added Ben, remembering Kelly's lopsided buns.

"There she is," said Jonathan, pointing.

Kelly was leaning against a sheep-pen, twisting her fingers in the fleece of a fat, sleepy ewe. The angles of her body were rigid, and the fierceness with which she twisted the fleece told Ben and Jonathan exactly how she was feeling.

"I saw you going into the tent," she said, as they leaned on the pen beside her.

"You can't win them all," said Ben.

"I don't win any," said Kelly.

"You will."

"Yes, at Grindlethorpe. I won't be beaten every time. I'm going to win the Lady Jiggins-Povey Cup. I absolutely, definitely am!"

She knotted the sheep's wool round her fingers, and stared at her brothers. She didn't want them to feel sorry for her. They'd got to believe what she said. Already her mind was making wild, rapid plans for Grindlethorpe Show.

"Come and have a hotdog," suggested Ben. He wished he could think of a way to help Kelly win that silver cup.

Chapter Two

The next afternoon, which was Sunday, Ben and Jonathan went to see Grandad.

"Your turn," Mum told them. "Kelly went last Sunday."

Kelly was buried in the Grindlethorpe Show programme, wondering how to win the Lady Jiggins-Povey Cup, so the boys had to go. They walked up the village street, past the smart converted barn belonging to William's family, and the neat white house where Rachel lived; and, just beyond the drive leading to Flora's Dad's farm, they reached Grandad's cottage.

Grandad had injured his legs in an accident, and couldn't get out much. He had a self-drive wheelchair, but he wasn't very good at managing it. Quite often it got out of control, ran the wrong way, and bumped into things; so mostly Grandad stayed indoors. But he hated being cooped up.

In the past he'd been a wonderful gardener. His roses and cabbages had been famous. They'd won dozens of prizes. Now weeds were taking over his garden, creeping across the cabbage beds and smothering the roses.

"Try and cheer him up," Dad had said, but it wasn't easy.

Ben and Jonathan talked about their holiday, and Grandad, who hadn't been away, looked glum. They talked about their favourite television programmes, and Grandad, who didn't watch any of them, looked bored. Jonathan felt stuck. He looked at Ben for a lead; and at last Ben remembered something which really interested Grandad.

"We went to Skelton Show yesterday," he said.

The old man's face brightened. "Who won the cup for the roses?" he asked.

"I'm afraid we didn't bother with the roses," Ben admitted. "We were looking at Kelly's things."

"Young Kelly!" Grandad leaned forward eagerly. "How many prizes did she win?"

It was an awkward question.

"None," said Ben.

"What — not one?"

Jonathan remembered Flora's words, and blurted them out.

"Wigglesworths never win anything," he said.

Grandad was more than interested now.

He was annoyed.

"Who says Wigglesworths never win? There was a time when that sideboard over there was loaded with silver cups. Groaning under the weight of them, it was."

"Jonathan's only eight," Ben apologized. "He's forgotten your cabbages and roses."

"And what about your Grandma's cakes and jam?" Grandad demanded. "And my father's pigs and sheep? And my grandfather's horses? They all won prizes." He sat up, straight and proud in his chair. "Once upon a time there wasn't much that the Wigglesworths didn't win. It's time your generation started winning again."

"Be fair. Your father had a farm," Ben pointed out. "And you've got a nice big garden. We've only got a little garden, and Dad hasn't a lot of time to work in it."

"And Mum never makes jam," Jonathan added. "She gets it at the supermarket."

Grandad didn't mind an argument; in fact, he enjoyed it. "Don't go blaming your parents. What about you young ones?"

"Like Ben said, Kelly keeps trying,"

answered Jonathan.

"Why doesn't she win, then?"

"Her things aren't terribly good," said Ben. "At least, other people's things are better."

"That's the trouble," said Jonathan. "Other people go on beating her."

"Time for a bit of jiggery-pokery," said Grandad.

The boys felt puzzled.

"What's jiggery-pokery?" asked Jonathan.

The proud look on Grandad's face changed into a mischievous smile.

"Almost every year," he began, "your Grandma's raspberry jam won first prize at Grindlethorpe Show. Then one summer, when all the jam was set out in the tent, people began to say that another pot — not your Grandma's — looked better. But when the judge took the top off that pot for a taste — judges do that, you know — a wasp flew out, and stung her nose. Well, now, a pot of jam with a wasp in it couldn't get first prize. So your Grandma's jam won again."

"How did the wasp get there?" Jonathan wondered.

Ben thought he knew.

Grandad went on looking mischievous.

"There were a lot of wasps about. Somebody could have caught one, and popped it under a jampot top. Jiggery-pokery often happens on the spur of the moment. I remember a class for heavy horses at Grindlethorpe Show when I was a lad. A farmer from twenty miles away brought his horse over. He said it was a famous champion. My old grandfather entered his own horse. He tipped me the wink, and I offered to hold this other one while the farmer got himself a glass of beer. Well, his horse was so fidgety in the ring, it hadn't a chance. My grandfather's horse won the Cup. And when that farmer got his champion horse home, he found it had a nettle under its tail. No wonder it wouldn't stand still!"

"You did it!" Jonathan shouted.

By now, Grandad was smiling broadly.

"I'm not saying anything. I'm only saying that a bit of jiggery-pokery never hurt the

Wigglesworths."

"Do you mean," questioned Ben, "that we should try a bit of jiggery-pokery for Kelly?"

Grandad wouldn't give a straight answer.

"It's all down to you. But we're wily, we Wigglesworths; wily and wiggly as serpents, people used to say. I took it as a compliment. They meant we were clever."

"I'm not wily, or wiggly, or clever," said Jonathan; but secretly he thought Ben might be.

Ben was silent, considering.

"Come and dig my garden one day soon," suggested Grandad. "You can do a lot of thinking with a spade in your hand."

Chapter Three

Kelly was studying the programme for the Grindlethorpe Show.

There were six classes for children under eleven, and whoever won the most would get the Lady Jiggins-Povey Cup. Kelly read the list over and over again:

Class 1 — Four jam tarts
Class 2 — An individual cold sweet
Class 3 — Handwriting
Class 4 — A decorated paper plate
Class 5 — A model animal made from fruit or vegetables
Class 6 — A country basket

Poor Kelly despaired. She couldn't see herself winning anything. Flora, who was a skilful cook as well as a good rider, would produce the best jam tarts and cold sweet. Artistic William would probably take first prizes for handwriting and the decorated paper plate. Rachel, who was neat-fingered, would make the cleverest animal and the prettiest basket.

Maybe I'll win six second prizes, thought Kelly. That would give me a good score.

But she knew she wouldn't. Rachel's cooking was better than hers; William would make a tidier model animal; and Flora had very elegant writing. They'd all get seconds and thirds when they didn't get firsts.

But I've got to beat them, thought Kelly. I really do want to win the Lady Jiggins-Povey Cup.

Once, she had seen an old photo at Grandad's. It showed his sideboard loaded with all the silver trophies he and Grandma had won. There were dozens of them; some tall, some wide, some with handles, some on polished stands.

"Wigglesworth cups!" Grandad had said proudly.

I don't want lots, thought Kelly. I just want the Lady Jiggins-Povey Cup.

She had seen it several times last year, placed prominently in the Kitsons' window. It was very pretty. It opened like a silver tulip on top of a slender stem. The names of all the winners were engraved on the side. 1988: Flora Sharp. 1989: Rachel Kitson. If only it could say 1990: Kelly Wigglesworth!

So which classes could she win? Kelly looked at the list again. If she made twenty jam tarts, surely four of them would be good enough for a prize; and handwriting just needed a bit of care. Then there was the country basket. What would she need for that? Just flowers, fruit, twigs, pebbles — anything that could be found in the countryside, attractively arranged in a basket. Easy! She only had to go and have a look.

Kelly tossed the programme on to the kitchen table, and set off.

Usually she ran everywhere, but now she made herself walk slowly. She went up a little winding lane, scanning the banks and hedges, feeling pleased with her own carefulness. It was August — rather late for wild flowers, but too early for berries. However, she picked some fluffy grasses and some harebells; and then she found a shiny magpie's feather. That was encouraging. She walked on.

The lane skirted the back of a field belonging to the Sharps. Flora's grey pony, Stardust, was grazing quietly. Flora was a good rider. She'd won lots of prizes with Stardust. If she'd only concentrate on the pony classes when she went to a show, and forget about cooking! But she liked to win everything she could.

Beyond the field was a stretch of woodland. Crossing it, Kelly was surprised to see a green caravan, half hidden in a thicket. It wasn't a place where people had camped before. If she hadn't been looking so hard for things, she might not even have noticed it.

She went closer, and saw footprints on some muddy ground near the caravan steps. The left shoe had a triangular patch on the heel. It showed up clearly in the mud.

Kelly shivered. There was something sinister about the caravan and the footprints. She turned away, and a sudden splash of colour caught her eye. In a clearing, some scarlet toadstools were growing. They were ruby-bright, and spotted with milky dots. Perfect for the country basket!

Kelly picked five. Then, in a fit of enthusiasm, she scratched up some deep green moss, lined the basket with it, and laid the toadstools in the middle. She arranged grasses and harebells around them, stuck the magpie's feather at one side — and there was her country basket! Stylish and unusual. She was sure it would win a prize.

She darted back across the wood, and down the winding lane.

All at once she heard a terrified screeching and squawking, as if a fox had got into a hen-run. And there had been some hens, outside Mrs Wooding's cottage, which was near Stardust's field. Kelly ran as fast as she could, thinking that, if there was a fox, she could

chase it away.

Round a twist in the lane, she almost bumped into a strange man.

"Sorry!" exclaimed Kelly.

He brushed past, clutching his coat, as if something was hidden under it. He hurried up the lane — and the print of a shoe with a triangular patch on the heel was left in the mud.

The caravan owner! What was he doing, Kelly wondered. But instantly she was distracted. There on the ground lay a brown hen's feather.

Just what I need for my basket, thought Kelly. She picked it up, and stuck it jauntily into the moss, opposite the magpie's feather. It felt warm, as if the hen had dropped it only a moment ago.

She remembered the fox, but the hens were quiet again. Whatever had disturbed them, had gone. Kelly skipped past them, and back into the village, brimming with satisfaction over her country basket.

Ben, or Rachel, or Flora, might have told her that she'd got it ready far too early. But,

with her usual impatience, Kelly didn't think
of that.

Chapter Four

It was the day before the Grindlethorpe Show, and Ben and Jonathan were digging Grandad's garden. With forks and spades they cut through the clods of earth, and filled a wheelbarrow with the docks, dandelions and thistles they'd uprooted.

Jonathan invented a little song which he sang to himself:

"We're wiping out the weeds.
We're wiping out the weeds.
Hey-ho, hey-ho,
We're wiping out the weeds."

But presently he was too puffed to sing, so he dug in silence.

Ben was silent too. He forked, and thought, and tossed dandelions into the wheelbarrow.

"Let's stop!" gasped Jonathan at last.

They stopped, and rested on the edge of the wheelbarrow, admiring the strip of ground

they'd cleared.

"Have you seen Kelly's decorated paper plate?" asked Ben.

"Yeah." Jonathan nodded.

"What did you think of it?"

"It's okay."

"Good enough to win?"

Jonathan considered. Kelly had coloured her plate yellow, drawn in two brown eyes and a black nose and whiskers, and sellotaped strands of yellow knitting wool rather untidily round the rim.

"What's it meant to be?" Jonathan had asked.

"A lion," said Kelly. "Can't you tell? The wool's its mane." And Jonathan saw that it was. But would other people know?

"It might just win, I s'pose," he told Ben cautiously.

"Rachel and William were talking in the shop, when I was buying some crisps," said Ben. "William's making his plate like a Hallowe'en lantern. He's cut big holes for the eyes, and glued shiny gold paper behind them."

"He's good at paper plates," sighed Jonathan.

"Rachel's sounded good too. Her plate's

going to be a witch's face. She said she was making a papier mâché nose and chin for it, and a witch's hat."

"Kelly's won't be as good as theirs," said Jonathan.

"That's what I wondered."

"Poor Kelly. It's really bad luck to be up against that lot. I mean, to have *three* people so much better than her."

"They're better at taking trouble. Kelly's a bit slapdash," said Ben severely.

"Poor Kelly," said Jonathan again. They sat on the wheelbarrow in silence, thinking about their sister.

"So what about some jiggery-pokery?" asked Ben presently.

"Stick nettles on the backs of the plates, you mean? Or put a wasp inside the witch's hat? We'd never be able to," said Jonathan.

"No. Something a bit different."

"What?"

"Wipe out the opposition, like we've wiped out the weeds. Kelly'd win, if Rachel and Flora and William weren't there."

"Brilliant!" exclaimed Jonathan. Then he

felt doubtful. "How?"

"I'm not sure," said Ben. "I'm still thinking. But if we could stop them even entering for the Show . . . " He picked up his fork, and began digging again.

Then there was a thump and a bump, and Grandad's wheelchair shot out of the open front door. He grabbed a bush to stop himself rolling away.

"Dratted thing!" he mumbled. "It's worse than a horse with a nettle under its tail. It won't do what I tell it. How much have you done?"

"Lots," said Ben, waving his fork over the newly-dug ground.

"Not bad. Not bad." Grandad steered his wheelchair erratically along the path. His sharp eyes peered in every direction. "Hey! You've been digging up my cabbages."

"We haven't," protested Jonathan.

"We can tell the difference between cabbages and dandelions," said Ben.

"Then where've they gone?"

Grandad pointed to the cabbage bed, and the boys saw gaps in the rows of cabbages.

"We haven't dug there yet," said Jonathan.

Grandad propelled the wheelchair nearer.

"No. I take it back. You haven't dug there yet," he said. "So it looks as if those cabbages have been stolen."

The boys rushed to inspect the cabbage bed.

"Who'd have done it?" asked Jonathan.

"I don't know, but there's a thief about. Mrs Wooding had a couple of hens stolen this week. Somebody took them, one at a time, and it wasn't a fox, because there was no mess. She thought somebody maybe wanted a bite to eat. Perhaps he fancied cabbage to go with his roast chicken."

"Were you going to send them to the Show?" asked Ben.

"No. My cabbages aren't what they were. I can't tend 'em like I used to. But I'll be at the Show myself."

"In your wheelchair? Will you be able to manage?" asked Ben.

Grandad was wobbling about, over the edge of the cabbage bed, and back on to the path, and a crowded showground was no place to be unsteady.

"I'll manage if you boys'll give me a bit of a hand," said Grandad. "It's going to be a fine day, and I'd hate to miss the Grindlethorpe Show."

Chapter Five

Kelly's twenty jam tarts were cooling on the kitchen table when the boys got home. Kelly was standing beside them, the ovencloth still in her hand.

"Do you like them?" she asked.

It was a difficult question. Kelly had slapped so much jam into some of them that it had boiled over, and run stickily down the sides. With others she had been cautious, and dabbed in a tiny spoonful of jam which had baked into a hard knob. Some tarts were all pastry, some were all jam. None of them was really right.

"That one's okayish." Jonathan pointed hopefully.

"It's not. It's drowning in jam," said Kelly.

"That one?"

"Yuck!"

"Well . . . " Jonathan paused. He and

Kelly stared at the twenty forlorn hopes.

"They're awful!" Kelly burst out. "They're really bad! I can't make jam tarts."

It was only too true. Her brothers couldn't argue.

"Try making another lot," suggested Ben.

"Oh, what's the good? They never work."

Ben looked at Jonathan. His lips shaped the words "jiggery-pokery". Jonathan nodded, and the two of them slipped out into the garden.

"I didn't say it aloud," explained Ben, "because I don't want Kelly to know we're helping her. But we've got to do something."

"Right," agreed Jonathan.

"While you were looking at the tarts," Ben went on, "I saw a glass of trifle on the fridge. She must have made it for her cold sweet."

"What was it like?"

"Lots of cherries on top, but the custard was a funny colour."

"So?"

"We're going on a few visits," said Ben.

He led the way up the village street. Bright orange posters were stuck on walls and in windows, announcing GRINDLETHORPE SHOW.

"As if people didn't know!" muttered Jonathan.

Ben strode past them, and on to the

converted barn, where William lived.

The yard in front, where farm carts had once unloaded hay, was now a smart patio, with paving stones, tubs of flowers, and a white metal table under a flowery umbrella. William, wearing white trousers and a striped shirt, was lounging on a sunbed, sipping fruit juice from a tall green glass.

Ben stopped to survey the patio, and Jonathan stopped too.

"D'you want something?" asked William, glancing up in surprise. His parents, rich newcomers to Grindlethorpe, had pointed out the children they thought he should make friends with, and they didn't include the Wigglesworths.

"No," said Ben. "I was just wondering what all this was for."

"All what?" said William.

"This paved bit. I mean, why not have a proper garden, and grow grass and cabbages."

"Cabbages! No, thank you." William wrinkled up his nose. "And when you're giving outdoor parties, ladies' heels mess up the grass, Mummy says."

"So you're going to be giving outdoor parties?" said Ben.

"Yes — really good ones," said William. "We'll do barbecued steaks and chickens, with lots of sauces. Mummy says the sauces *make* a barbecue. Daddy'll do the wine."

"Will we be invited?"

William looked surprised again. "I don't think so. They'll be for special friends."

"Thanks a million," muttered Jonathan.

"Well, that's lucky. I hate parties," said Ben cheerfully. "Have you made your things for the Show? Can we see them?"

William must be pleased with them, Jonathan decided, or he wouldn't have bothered to uncurl himself from the sunbed, and lead the way inside, through a spacious hall, to a white-painted dining room.

"There!" said William.

On the table lay a long poem, copied in a beautiful italic script; the Hallowe'en lantern plate with its gold eyes twinkling; four crisp tarts filled with greengage jam; and a mouse made out of a pear, with slivers of carrot for ears, redcurrants for eyes, and a curling daisy tail.

"Wow!" exclaimed Jonathan before he could stop himself. He was impressed.

"I've still got to make an apple snow for my cold sweet, and finish my country basket," said William. "I'm plaiting a wreath of roses to go round it."

"Poor William. I'm sorry for you," said Ben.

Once more, William looked astonished, and a bit cross too. "Why?"

"Playing with flowers, and making dainty little tarts. Honestly! Are you going to ballet lessons too?"

"Shut up! Don't be so rude," said William.

"I don't mean to be rude. I'm just warning you. You're new to the country. These fancy things may be okay in towns, but, in the country, boys are tough. They don't go round making puddings."

"I want to win the Cup," said William.

"But it's a Cup that girls always win. Have you seen the names on the side? Flora Sharp. Rachel Kitson. William Edge'll look pretty daft at the end of the list."

"Will it?"

"Yes. That's why I never went in for the Lady Jiggins-Povey Cup," Ben explained. "I'm too old now. I'm twelve. When I was your age, I'd probably have won. Only I didn't want to look silly."

"Mummy wants me to win," said William.

"Mummy!" Ben repeated the word scornfully. "Well, we can't stop. Come on, Jonathan. Enjoy plaiting your roses, William."

"And if he doesn't back out after that," he murmured to Jonathan, as they crossed the patio, "I'll eat his fancy writing, and his paper plate, too."

Chapter Six

A little further up the village street was the neat white house where Rachel lived.

Rachel's mother was standing at the gate, listening to William's mother. Mrs Edge seemed to have a great deal to say.

"I'm sure William can win the Lady Jiggins-Povey Cup," she was explaining. "He must be the most artistic child in Grindlethorpe. You country people have had things your own way for a long time, but newcomers like us bring in fresh talent. I think you'll find that Lady Jiggins-Povey will be impressed when she sees William's work."

"Lady Jiggins-Povey likes things done the old way," retorted Mrs Kitson. "I should know, seeing she gave my Rachel the Cup last time."

"I daresay she'll change her views when she sees what a really gifted child can do," said

Mrs Edge; and the glint in her eye seemed to add — "She'd better!"

Ben strolled up to them. Jonathan followed, wondering what jiggery-pokery was in store. Ben was giving nothing away.

"Hello, Mrs Kitson," he said cheerfully. "Is Rachel ready for the Show?"

Mrs Kitson turned away from Mrs Edge with relief.

"Oh, yes. She's showing her things to Flora. Go in, and have a look."

The girls were in the kitchen. On the table were four tarts filled with strawberry jam; a little dish of chocolate mousse; a neatly copied poem; a paper plate topped with a witch's hat, and sprouting a hooked nose and chin; a basket heaped with coloured fruits; and a ladybird made from a tiny tomato, with French bean legs and currant spots.

Behind them, Rachel had placed the Lady Jiggins-Povey Cup. She had polished it to a beautiful sheen; and her name twinkled in the sunlight, at the bottom of the prizewinners' list.

"I don't see why I shouldn't win it again," she was saying.

"Your writing's a bit uneven," Flora pointed out.

"Well — I don't mind William winning the handwriting class."

"And your witch's nose isn't straight."

"Witch's noses shouldn't be straight," said Ben. He walked into the kitchen, and picked up the paper plate. "Very good, Rachel. Have you finished your things, Flora?"

"It's none of your business," snapped Flora.

"She's done everything except the cooking," said Rachel helpfully. "She's leaving that till this evening. She's got to groom Stardust for the riding classes first."

"Isn't it risky, leaving the cooking so late?" said Ben.

"No, it's not," said Flora. "Grooming doesn't take long, unless Stardust's very muddy, which he won't be. What are you and Jonathan doing here, anyway? Are you spying for Kelly?"

"No," said Ben. "I don't think Kelly's got much chance; not now I've seen Rachel's things."

"Do you think I'll really win?" asked Rachel, looking pleased.

"Quite likely. The problem is," said Ben, "that, if you do, the Edges will be mad at you."

"Why?"

"Mrs Edge wants William to have the Cup. And you know what she's like! Edgy as her name; prickly as an 'edge'og."

"Hedgehog," corrected Rachel. She looked thoughtful. "Won't it be good enough for her if William wins the writing class, and maybe the paper plates? I suppose my witch's nose should have been straighter."

Ben gave a little laugh. "I'm sorry, Rachel. It's the Cup or nothing for William. The Edges don't do things by halves. It's like these parties they're planning on their patio. Have you heard about them? There'll be barbecued steaks and chickens, and dozens of fancy sauces. The whole works!"

"Honestly?" Rachel's eyes were round. "Wouldn't it be great to go?"

"But they'll only ask people they like; and they'll hate anyone who's beaten little William. Still," finished Ben, "it's down to you. Come on, Jonathan. We've a job to do."

He swept Jonathan out of the room, and into the village street.

"Wow!" exclaimed Jonathan, once they were out of earshot. "That was terrific. You've made Rachel think that if she wins the Cup, she won't be asked to William's parties."

"Right," agreed Ben. "And she's sure her things are good enough to win again. So what d'you think she'll do?"

"Drop out."

"Yes. And won't she be fed up when she finds little William's dropped out too!"

Ben chuckled as he hurried along.

"What's this job we're doing? Where are we going?" asked Jonathan.

"We'll fetch a metal bucket first," said Ben, "and we'll fill it with nasty, smelly mud. We might get some round the Sharps' cattle trough, if nobody's looking. Then we'll give Stardust a nice mud bath. And then Flora'll be so busy grooming him, she won't have time for her cooking."

They scraped up a bucket of mud without anyone seeing them, and carried it up to Stardust's field. The grey pony had a friendly nature. When they called, he trotted up to the gate by the lane.

"You hold him," Ben told Jonathan. "I'll plaster the mud on."

"Yuck!" said Jonathan, trying not to breathe through his nose.

Ben tried not to notice the smell too, as he rubbed handfuls of mud into the pony's grey coat. Stardust seemed to enjoy the attention.

He stood as still as a rock.

"This'll take some brushing off!" remarked Ben, with satisfaction.

"Hey!" cried a voice.

Looking up, they saw Flora coming into the field through another gate.

"What are you doing to my pony?" she shouted.

"Run!" commanded Ben.

Flinging the empty bucket into some nettles, he dashed up the lane. Jonathan zipped after him, and they made for the shelter of the little wood beyond the field.

Chapter Seven

Ben and Jonathan crouched behind some brambles. Their hearts were pounding.

"Did Flora see who we were?" whispered Jonathan.

"Dunno. We were a long way off."

"Is she coming after us?"

They listened intently, but there were no following footsteps. It was very quiet in the wood. The branches rustled a little, but that was all.

"Anyway," hissed Ben, "if she comes chasing us, she'll waste even more of her cooking time!"

That made Jonathan giggle so much, he had to stuff his fingers in his mouth to stop himself laughing aloud.

Still nobody came. Presently they dared to move a little, and talk in normal voices. Ben cleaned his hands with several large dock leaves.

"Shall we go home?" asked Jonathan.

"Better wait a bit longer. Flora might still be in the field."

"Will she be grooming Stardust there?"

"She might be. We can't chance it."

"All that yucky mud!" And Jonathan chuckled again.

"I bet Kelly'll win the Cup now," said Ben.

"The Lady Jiggins-Povey Cup," said Jonathan solemnly. "Wow! Grandad'll be pleased."

"He'll think it's great to see a Wigglesworth's name on the side," said Ben.

"Is it really valuable?" asked Jonathan. "Did it cost a lot?"

"Sure to have done. Lady Jiggins-Povey's very rich. It's probably the most valuable Cup in the show."

"Worth having, then?"

"You bet! Ssh! What's that?"

Someone was running up the lane. Ducking behind the brambles, the boys froze. The hurrying feet came nearer.

"It's not Flora. It's Kelly!" exclaimed Ben.

Sure enough, their sister came running

towards them. She looked worried and cross.

"Hi, Kelly! What are you doing?" called Jonathan.

Kelly was so startled, she nearly dropped the basket she was carrying.

"Jonathan! You little wretch! You gave me a terrible fright."

"You gave us one."

"Why? What are you hiding there for?"

Ben had no intention of letting Kelly find out about their jiggery-pokery. "Just a bit of fun. Nothing really. What are you doing?"

Kelly's face clouded again.

"I picked some toadstools here the other day — lovely red and white ones. They were for my country basket. But I got them much too early, and when I looked at my basket just now, they had all gone wrinkled and dry. They looked horrid." She sighed. "Why do all my things go wrong? I thought I'd a chance with those toadstools. So I came to see if there were any left."

"Whereabouts were they?"

"Not far from here. Past the caravan."

"What caravan?"

"Just behind you. Haven't you seen it? You must be blind!"

The boys turned, and noticed for the first time the green caravan, half buried in the bushes a few feet away. It had a lurking, sinister look.

"Does somebody live there?" whispered Jonathan.

"I think so." Kelly was whispering too. "A man with a triangular patch on his shoe. I saw his footprint."

"That's funny," began Jonathan, "because—"

"Look!" Ben interrupted. "Over there. Toadstools!"

"Good!" said Kelly; for the scarlet toadstools splashed with white were scattered all over a clearing nearby. Kelly chose several of the largest.

"Put them in the fridge overnight," advised Ben. "That'll keep them fresh."

"My feathers are okay," said Kelly. "I'm going to have feathers, toadstools, grass and moss."

Ben thought of William's plaited rose wreath, and Rachel's beautiful coloured fruits. It was lucky they'd wiped out the opposition.

"Did you see Flora in Stardust's field?" he asked casually.

"No."

So it was safe to go home. And at last Jonathan could tell them what Ben had interrupted.

"You know that shoe print with the triangular patch Kelly saw by the caravan? Well, I saw one too. In Grandad's garden."

"When?" asked Ben.

"Just after he told us about his cabbages being nicked."

Ben stood still. "You mean, the man in the caravan could be the thief?"

"Yes. Shall we go back, and see if he's cooking cabbage?"

"We wouldn't be able to prove it was Grandad's cabbage. Still," said Ben, "we might investigate a bit, after the Show."

"Why were you hiding by the caravan? You still haven't told me," said Kelly.

"Oh," said Ben, "we were just chatting about how valuable the Lady Jiggins-Povey Cup is, and how you're going to win it tomorrow."

Chapter Eight

They woke to sunshine on the morning of the
Show. Kelly got up early, and when Ben and
Jonathan came down, all her things were
arranged on a tray, ready to take to the Show.

"What's the cucumber doing?" asked Jonathan.

"It's my vegetable-animal. Can't you see? It's a crocodile. The trouble is," said Kelly, "that I haven't cut its mouth right. I put in a bit of tomato for the tongue, and it keeps sliding out."

"Make the mouth bigger," advised Ben.

He was thankful that the cucumber-crocodile wouldn't be up against William's pear-mouse, or Rachel's tomato-ladybird. They'd really been much better.

"What do you think of my things?" asked Kelly, eyeing them anxiously, for their faults were only too obvious to her. "Should I put a bit more wool on the lion's mane?"

"They're fine," said Ben. "Don't start messing about with them now." He winked at Jonathan behind Kelly's back.

"You've done your best, love, and that's what counts," said Mum.

"I could eat your trifle now," said Dad. "It looks delicious."

"Do you really and truly mean it?" said Kelly.

"Of course I do," said Dad.

"Where'll we put the Cup, when Kelly brings it home?" asked Jonathan.

"The sideboard's the proper place," said Dad.

"I shall clear a big space for it," said Mum.

Ben and Jonathan were going to take Grandad and his wheelchair to the Show, so Dad drove Kelly and her tray of things to the field where it was held. The entries for the competitions had to arrive early, so that they could be judged before any spectators were allowed into the tents.

"Good luck, Kelly," said Dad. "I hope you win lots of red cards."

And the Lady Jiggins-Povey Cup, thought Kelly, climbing carefully out of the car with her tray.

She walked across the field to a big tent, labelled HANDICRAFTS. Crowds of people were milling about inside, under the white canvas, arranging their cakes, and pots of jam, and bottles of homemade wine, on the long tables.

"Children's classes down that side," directed a man, wearing a badge saying

"Show Official".

Kelly walked across the tent.

Grouped by the children's table were Rachel, Flora and William. Their heads were close together, as if they were deep in conversation.

"There she is!" exclaimed Flora, suddenly glancing up.

Rachel and William looked up too. They all stared fiercely at Kelly, and Kelly suddenly felt alarmed. What was the matter?

"What do you think you were doing, Kelly Wigglesworth, plotting against us?" demanded Flora.

"Cheat!" said Rachel.

"Slimy snake!" said William.

Kelly nearly dropped the tray. She gazed in bewilderment at the three angry faces.

"What do you mean? I don't get it!"

"You do!" snapped Flora. "So don't pretend. You made your horrible brothers try to trick us out of entering for the Show, so that you could win for a change. Well, bad luck! We've foiled them!"

"What?" Kelly felt as if the tent was spinning round her.

Rachel took over the explaining. "Ben and

Jonathan said it would upset William's family if I went in for the Lady Jiggins-Povey Cup and beat him; and they told William he'd be a drip if he tried. And then they smeared mud all over Stardust, so that Flora'd be too busy grooming him to finish her things. But Flora saw them, so she got her Dad to brush Stardust, and she came and told William and me what had happened, and then we saw through your brothers' nasty plans," finished Rachel, with her most self-satisfied, kitty-cat smile.

"They weren't very clever," sneered Flora.

"They were dead stupid," said William.

"I didn't know anything about it — and I still don't understand," faltered Kelly.

"Oh, go and ask Ben and Jonathan," said Rachel impatiently. "Go and tell them their silly ideas were a big flop."

"As if Kelly's things *could* win," gibed Flora, glancing at Kelly's tray. And, out of her own basket, she took four beautiful, flaky tarts, each filled with a different coloured jam; a pink meringue, with piped swirls of cream; a cucumber crocodile, with goggling carrot eyes, and a long carrot tongue . . . another crocodile, far better than hers!

And Kelly, staring, suddenly knew why she never won. She wasn't careful, as the three others were. She dashed at things. She picked her toadstools too early, and slapped jam haphazardly into her tarts.

Next time, she thought, I'll be really calm and careful. But there won't be another time, because now she was ten. Rachel, or William, or Flora, was going to win the Cup.

"Just a minute, you kids," came a loud voice. "Hold on."

The man with the official badge was striding towards them. He had a white tablecloth in his hands. He shook it out with a flourish, and spread it over all the children's entries, hiding them completely.

"Why are you doing that?" cried Flora.

"I'm afraid there's been a hitch," said the man. "These classes may not be judged."

"Why not?" Rachel and Flora asked together.

"Somebody's stolen the Lady Jiggins-

Povey Cup."

The children gazed at him with horror.

"But we brought it to the Show this morning," protested Rachel.

"I know. And your father left it at the secretary's tent, with all the other trophies. But, somehow, a thief managed to slip in, and pinch it. Just that one cup — as if he knew how valuable it was! We've alerted the police."

What a shock! Kelly felt as if she'd swallowed a very cold ice cream too quickly. She forgot the others, and their strange complaints about Ben and Jonathan. That beautiful silver cup had gone . . . She couldn't stand still. Leaving the others, she rushed away, over the grass to the secretary's tent.

Quite a crowd had gathered, exclaiming and asking questions.

"Bad security," they told each other. They pointed to the table on which the other trophies stood — cups for roses and cabbages, horses and sheep.

Kelly looked down, and saw, on the muddy grass, the print of a shoe, with a triangular patch on the heel.

Then, in her quick brain, things began to come together. She remembered how, yesterday, she'd found her brothers in the wood. They'd told her they'd been discussing the Lady Jiggins-Povey Cup, and how valuable it was.

And they'd been just beside the caravan. Anyone inside could have heard them. And if that person was already into stealing cabbages, or even hens . . .

Kelly knew what had happened, and she didn't stop to think any more. She whisked over to the gate of the field, where a policeman was just climbing into his panda car.

"Please," she called, "I think I know where you'll find the Lady Jiggins-Povey Cup."

Chapter Nine

The news that the Lady Jiggins-Povey Cup had been stolen, buzzed round the showground.

"Well, well," remarked Grandad. "It sounds like a bit of jiggery-pokery to me. Come on, you boys. Own up." And he looked from Ben on one side of his wheelchair to Jonathan on the other.

"It wasn't us," protested Jonathan.

"We wouldn't do anything like that," said Ben.

"If you had, you wouldn't be the first," said Grandad. "I remember people making cups disappear so their rivals couldn't get 'em."

"Stealing them, you mean?" asked Jonathan.

"Only temporarily," said Grandad. "They generally turned up later." He chuckled mischievously, and nearly ran over Ben's toes.

"Watch out!" snapped Ben. He felt very annoyed about the Lady Jiggins-Povey Cup. After all they'd done, was it not going to be there for Kelly to win?

"They'll find it," said Grandad airily. "Now, how about going to see what young Kelly's been making?"

But they took a long time to reach the Handicrafts tent. Grandad was enjoying his outing, and he had to stop and peer into the sheep-pens, inspect the poultry, toss some balls at a coconut shy, and visit the flower and vegetable tent to see what the roses and cabbages were like.

"We may as well give 'em time to find the Cup," he said, when Ben and Jonathan tried to hurry him.

"Suppose they don't find it?" said Jonathan, and he grabbed an armrest to stop Grandad's wheelchair running over a silky sheepdog.

"That wheelchair's a danger to the public," muttered Ben, who was still feeling cross.

They were too busy with the cabbages to

see Kelly's triumphant return to the Show. The panda car bumped over the grass to a tent labelled MEMBERS ONLY, where the important people had gathered.

"You knew where to find it? You clever girl!" exclaimed Lady Jiggins-Povey.

She was nice, thought Kelly. Although she was so rich, her clothes were quite ordinary, and her face was kind.

"Yes, Kelly led us straight to a caravan in the woods," explained the policeman. "The man inside must have seen us coming, because he burst out, and ran away. I left one of my constables chasing him. We went into the caravan, and the Cup was hidden under a rug on the bunk."

"Is it damaged?" asked Lady Jiggins-Povey.

"Not a scratch; not a dent." The policeman held it out for her to see.

"And who was the man who had taken it?"

"Well, lurking in the woods like that, I'd say he was on the run from the law," said the policeman. "He seems to have been living rough. If he'd heard about your Cup

somehow, he might have thought he'd take it,
and sell it for cash. He probably had no
money."

"But we've got it back, thanks to Kelly,"
said Lady Jiggins-Povey. "And I must go
straight over, and judge the children's classes.
Come along, my dear."

But Kelly hung back. Remembering Rachel, and Flora, and William, her heart had sunk like a stone. She wondered why she had bothered to save the Cup, since one of them would now win it. As usual, she had acted on the spur of the moment; and, once again, she wished she hadn't.

"Is something the matter?" Lady Jiggins-Povey asked her.

"Not really. I was just thinking about my entries — my tarts and my crocodile, and all the rest of them. They aren't very good," said Kelly sadly.

Grandad, Ben and Jonathan had reached the Handicrafts tent, when the news went flying round.

"The Cup's been found! The Lady Jiggins-Povey Cup!"

"What did I tell you?" demanded Grandad.

An official strode past, and tweaked off the tablecloth which had been covering the children's entries.

"Oh, no!" exclaimed Ben. "Kelly isn't going to win, after all!"

For there on the table, plain and unmistakable, were William's pear-mouse and Rachel's tomato-ladybird, far outshining Kelly's cucumber-crocodile. Three sets of beautiful jam tarts put Kelly's to shame; while, even with its glowing toadstools, Kelly's country basket looked a mess beside Rachel's heap of fruit, William's plaited rose wreath, and Flora's dainty arrangement of ferns and shiny pebbles.

"Those are Rachel's things!" shrieked Jonathan. "And William's! And are those Flora's? They shouldn't be here."

"But they are," said Ben grimly.

"What's this?" Grandad wheeled his chair alongside the table. "What's wrong?"

"Our jiggery-pokery," groaned Ben. "It hasn't worked."

"Lady Jiggins-Povey's coming!" someone shouted.

The crowd parted a little. Lady Jiggins-Povey, with a bunch of officials, came walking down the tent.

"Kelly!" gasped Ben, astonished.

Their sister was trailing behind the

important people, looking as if she wished she wasn't there. But Lady Jiggins-Povey turned, and took her arm.

Ben and Jonathan were so surprised, that they didn't notice exactly what happened next. Perhaps Grandad tried to turn the wheelchair. Perhaps it just ran out of control by itself. There was a crash, and a bang, and the whole table collapsed. Meringues and trifle, paper plates and toadstools, jam tarts and cucumbers, flew through the air, and splattered down on the grass.

"Dratted wheelchair! Must have hit a table leg," mumbled Grandad, wiping custard off his trousers.

And there was a long pause, while everybody stared at the ruin of the children's classes.

Lady Jiggins-Povey rose to the occasion.

"Dear me! It looks as if I can't award my Cup in the usual way this year. What a shame! I can see some former prize-winners here, as well as some newcomers, and I can guess how good their things were." And she smiled at Rachel, Flora, and William. "But there's no harm in a change now and then, and someone at this Show particularly deserves a reward. Ladies and gentlemen, I am presenting my Cup, not for handicrafts, but for quick wit and prompt action. Kelly Wigglesworth saved the Cup, and she must have it."

"Me!" gasped Kelly.

And, as she took the Cup, and touched its shining surface, she saw the nicest thing of all — Rachel, Flora, and William, were all clapping and smiling, as if they were really pleased for her.

The Cup shone in splendour on the Wigglesworths' sideboard.

"It's only right that Kelly should have it," said Mum. "Flora and Rachel have each had their turn, and William's a year younger, so he can win it next year."

"I might go in for it," said Jonathan. "It could be fun."

"What I'm wondering," said Ben, "is whether Grandad did it on purpose."

"Knocked over the table? I wouldn't put it past him," said Dad, "though he won't admit it."

"I think I shall call it the Jiggery-Pokery Cup," said Ben.

Kelly didn't hear a word they were saying. She gazed and gazed at the beautiful silver Cup, with her name on it at last.

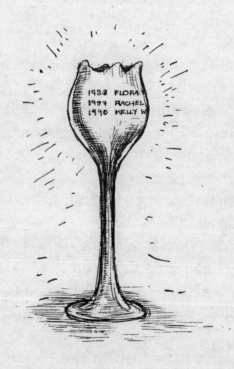

JUGGLERS

There are books to suit everyone in Hippo's JUGGLERS series:

When I Lived Down Cuckoo Lane
by Jean Wills   £1.75
A small girl and her family move into a new house in Cuckoo Lane. Follow her adventures through the year as she makes friends, starts a new school, learns to ride a bike, and even helps out at her father's shop.

The Secret of Bone Island by Sam McBratney   £1.75
Linda, Peter and Gareth are very curious about Bone Island. Especially when they're told some weird stories about the island's history. And then three suspicious-looking men warn them to stay away from the island . . .

Stan's Galactic Bug by John Emlyn Edwards   £1.75
Stan can't believe his eyes when his computer game traps an alien from outer space. It's up to Stan to save the intergalactic traveller from destruction!

As If By Magic by Jo Furminger   £1.75
Natasha has never seen a girl as weird as Harriet – the new girl in the class. But not only does she *look* strange, with her dark tatty clothes and bright green eyes, but the oddest things start to happen when she's around.

Look out for these other titles in the JUGGLERS series:

Bags of Trouble by Michael Harrison

STREAMERS

We've got lots of great books for younger readers in Hippo's STREAMERS series:

Sally Ann – On Her Own by Terrance Dicks £1.75
Sally Ann is a very special toy. She's a rag doll who likes to be involved in everything that's going on. When Sally Ann finds out that the nursery school where she lives might be closed down, she decides it's time to take action!

Sally Ann – The School Play by Terrance Dicks £1.75
When the nursery school's electricity goes off, Sally Ann comes up with a wonderful idea to pay for the new wiring. But not everything runs as smoothly as Sally Ann would like!

The Little Yellow Taxi and His Friends
by Ruth Ainsworth £1.75
The little grey car can't get to sleep at night, and keeps all the other cars and lorries awake. So the garage owner paints the little car yellow, gives him a sign for his roof, and turns him into an all-night taxi.

Tom by Ruth Silvestre £1.75
The circus has come to town, and Tom tries to tell his parents about it. But they are always too busy to listen. . . A delightful collection of stories about Tom, his family and friends.

Look out for these other titles in the STREAMERS series:

Nate the Great by Marjorie Sharmat
Nate the Great and the Missing Key by Marjorie Sharmat

HIPPO CLASSICS

HIPPO CLASSICS is a series of some of the best-loved books for children.

Black Beauty by Anna Sewell £1.50
Black Beauty is a magnificent horse: sweet-tempered, strong and courageous, coloured bright black with one white foot and a white star on his forehead. His adventures during his long and exciting life make one of the most-loved animal stories ever written.

Alice's Adventures in Wonderland
by Lewis Carroll £1.50
When Alice sees the White Rabbit scurry by, her curiosity gets the better of her and she follows him down a rabbit hole. Suddenly she finds herself in an extraordinary world of mad tea parties, grinning Cheshire cats, lobster quadrilles and many more wonderful scenes and characters.

Wind in the Willows by Kenneth Grahame £1.50
One spring day Mole burrows out of the ground and makes his way to the river. There he meets Water Rat and is introduced to all Ratty's friends – Badger, Otter and the loveable and conceited Toad. There's an adventure-filled year ahead for all the animals in this classic story.

Kidnapped by R L Stevenson £1.50
David Balfour is cheated of his rightful estate and then brutally kidnapped. He manages to escape – but is forced to go on the run again when he's wrongfully accused of murder. An action-packed tale of treachery and danger.

The Railway Children by E Nesbit £1.50
The lives of Roberta, Peter and Phyllis are changed completely after the dreadful evening when their father is taken away. They move to the country, where they miss their friends and parties and trips to the zoo. Then they discover the nearby railway, and soon the children find their days filled with adventure.

Treasure Island by R L Stevenson £1.50
When Jim Hawkins opens up Captain Flint's old sea chest, he is amazed to find a treasure map inside it. This discovery plunges him into a series of extraordinary adventures involving pirates, shipwreck, mutiny and murder, on his long and dangerous search for the island and its treasure.

A Christmas Carol by Charles Dickens £1.50
It's Christmas Eve, and as usual Scrooge is hard at work in his counting house, sneering at the good cheer and charitable spirit of people celebrating the festive season. But then the mean old man is visited by the Ghosts of Christmas Past, Christmas Present and Christmas Yet to Come, and he undergoes an amazing transformation.

Little Women by L M Alcott £1.50
Times are hard for the March sisters, with their father away at war and the family's lack of money. But the girls – Meg, Jo, Beth and Amy – let their enthusiasm and good nature shine through their troubles, and bring gaiety and hope to their own lives and those of the people around them.

White Fang by Jack London £1.50
In the frozen wastelands of north-west Canada, White Fang is born. Half-wolf, half-dog, he is the strongest and only survivor of the litter. And his strength and ferocity is put to the test again and again in this savage world where men and animals alike fight for survival.

Robinson Crusoe by Daniel Defoe £1.50
Shipwrecked on an uninhabited island, Robinson Crusoe has little hope of rescue or survival. But little by little he builds up a home for himself on the island. And then, after twelve years of solitude, he discovers footprints in the sand . . .

HIPPO BOOKS FOR OLDER READERS

If you enjoy a really good read, look out for all the
Hippo books that are available right now. You'll find
gripping adventure stories, romance novels, spooky
ghost stories and all sorts of fun fiction to keep you
glued to your book!

HAUNTINGS: Ghost Abbey by Robert Westall £1.95
The Little Vampire in Love
by Angela Sommer-Bodenberg   £1.25
Snookered by Michael Hardcastle   £1.50
Palace Hill by Peter Corey   £1.95
Black Belt by Nicholas Walker   £1.75
STEPSISTERS 1: The War Between the
Sisters by Tina Oaks   £1.75
THE MALL 1: Setting Up Shop
by Carolyn Sloan   £1.75
Conrad's War by Andrew Davies   £1.75
Cassie Bowen Takes Witch Lessons by Anna
Grossnickle Hines   £1.75
Tales for the Midnight Hour by J B Stamper £1.75

You'll find these and many more fun Hippo books at
your local bookshop, or you can order them direct. Just
send off to *Customer Services, Hippo Books, Westfield
Road, Southam, Leamington Spa, Warwickshire CV33
0JH*, not forgetting to enclose a cheque or postal order
for the price of the book(s) plus 30p per book for postage
and packing.

HAUNTINGS by Hippo Books is a new series of excellent ghost stories for older readers.

Ghost Abbey by Robert Westall
When Maggie and her family move into a run-down old abbey, they begin to notice some very strange things going on in the rambling old building. Is there any truth in the rumour that the abbey is haunted?

Don't Go Near the Water by Carolyn Sloan
Brendan knew instinctively that he shouldn't go near Blackwater Lake. Especially that summer, when the water level was so low. But what was the dark secret that lurked in the depths of the lake?

Voices by Joan Aiken
Julia had been told by people in the village that Harkin House was haunted. And ever since moving in to the house for the summer, she'd been troubled by violent dreams. What had happened in the old house's turbulent past?

The Nightmare Man by Tessa Krailing
Alex first sees the man of his darkest dreams at Stackfield Pond. And soon afterwards he and his family move in to the old house near the pond — End House — and the nightmare man becomes more than just a dream.

A Wish at the Baby's Grave by Angela Bull
Desperate for some money, Cathy makes a wish for some at the baby's grave in the local cemetery. Straight afterwards, she finds a job at an old bakery. But there's something very strange about the bakery and the two Germans who work there. . .

The Bone-Dog by Susan Price
Susan can hardly believe her eyes when her uncle Bryan makes her a pet out of an old fox-fur, a bone and some drops of blood — and then brings it to life. It's wonderful to have a pet which follows her every command — until the bone-dog starts to obey even her unconscious thoughts. . .

The Old Man on a Horse by Robert Westall
Tobias couldn't understand what was happening. His parents and little sister had gone to Stonehenge with the hippies, and his father was arrested. Then his mother disappeared. But while sheltering with his sister in a barn, he finds a statue of an old man on a horse, and Tobias and Greta find themselves transported to the time of the Civil War...

The Rain Ghost by Garry Kilworth
What is the secret of the old, rusty dagger Steve finds while on a school expedition? As soon as he brings it home, the ancient-looking knife is connected with all sorts of strange happenings. And one night Steve sees a shadowy, misty figure standing in the pouring rain, watching the house...

The Haunting of Sophie Bartholomew by Elizabeth Lindsay
Sophie hates the house she and her mother have moved to in Castle Street. It's cold and dark and very frightening. And when Sophie hears that it's supposed to be haunted, she decides to investigate...

Picking Up the Threads by Ian Strachan
There's something strange going on at the rambling old house where Nicky is spending her holidays with her great-aunt. In the middle of the night, Nicky is woken up by the sound of someone crying for help. But when she goes to investigate, there's nobody there!

The Wooden Gun by Elizabeth Beresford
Kate is very unhappy on the Channel Island where she's spending her summer holidays. She senses a mysterious, forbidding atmosphere, but no one else seems to notice it. Is it just her imagination, or does the beautiful, sun-drenched island hide a dark secret?